THE MYSTERY OF HUMANOID ROBOTS

S. SHAWN JEHAFIEL

ISBN 979-888546152-8

To my parents and to my sister for always loving and supporting me.

Contents

The Mystery of Humanoid Robots

Master Shawn- My grandson little boy has written a story book. When he briefed the story few months back, I wondered how it is possible as story writing is certainly a big task. Now-a-days reading habit among the students is on the decline. However, I appreciate his parents for extending their tacit support to achieve such goal. I wish him to write more and more and his writings may stand as light house to the society.

Grandparents
Mr.S.Mangalaraja Sargunar, M.A.,Rtd S.I
Mrs.M.Jebakani Sargunar, M.A.,

Wishes and Blessings, Shawn Jehafiel.

Grandparents
Mr.S.Selvaraj, Rtd H.M.,
Mrs.P.Gnanamani Radhabai, Rtd H.M.,

At the age of 11, kids will ask robot toys or stories to be narrated by parents but it's a great achievement to narrate a story by you and publish it as well. Congrats Shawn for your creativity and motivation from your parents. Keep rocking!

Uncle
M.Josef Raja Hemanth Sargunar, MBA.,
CEO, Enter2job, Malaysia.

We wish you good luck and God bless you in abundance. Be a blessing to all.

Parents
Er. S.Sudhrson Rajkumar, M.E.,
Dr.M.Beulah Hemalatha, Ph.d.,
S. Snowlyn Juanita, UKG

Acknowledgements

I thank the Lord God Almighty for helping me to write a story on robots. I would like to acknowledge with gratitude the support and love of my family- my parents, S.Sudharson and M. Hema; my sister, S.Snowlyn; my grandparents, S. Mangalaraja grandpa and M.Jebakani granny; my uncle, M.Josef Raja Hemanth; my grandparents, Radha Bai granny and Selvaraj grandpa. They all kept me going, and this book would not have been possible without them.

I convey my thanks to the Principal, Dr.N.K.Charles, The Vikasa School, Sawyerpuram, Tuticorin for rendering me immense support.

I owe my hearty thanks to my teachers Mrs.C.Amutha B.SC.,B.Ed., and Mrs.P.Vasuki, Librarian of The Vikasa School, Sawyerpuram, Tuticorin for emboldening me.

My thanks to the Notion Press Publishing Team for fostering a sense of support.

S.Shawn Jehafiel,
VI Std,
The Vikasa School, Sawyerpuram.

Prologue

During the pandemic, I had an interest to make robots and understood that it was not that easy. Humans are thinking that artificial intelligence is better. We are just wasting our time and dependent on that. We have our own intelligence but we are not using to the core. From my Tamil lesson, I learnt that **Robot** means **'a slave'**. So, I want to explain people that we create such machines, programme it and that do whatever we instruct. They cannot help us in every situation. But humans can. Let us work hard, save nature and do our best.

S.Shawn Jehafiel,
VI Std.

Robot Heart Copy

CHAPTER ONE

Once there was a little lab in the hamlet of Tokyo. In that Lab, so many robots were there in the secret digital password room that was made of steel. The password was **Robot Heart Copy**. There Dr.Sunehoro, Dr.Ganma and Dr.Jinakkafu were robot scientists. Dr.Sunehoro was a good scientist. He was from a small town and had a dream to help people by the robots. So, he made robots for a good cause. He served food to the orphans and the needy with the help of his robots. He became famous and was recognized as the best robot scientist in Tokyo. He also taught the formula of making robots to Ganma and Jinakkafu. But they were jealous of Sunehoro's activities. They all worked together but Ganma and Jinakkafu had their own humanoid robots in the lab. Ganma considered Jinakkafu as his role model but not so venomous like his master. He was much interested to do novel robots and wished to be the best robot scientist. But Jinakkafu's plan was to take the control of the robots in Tokyo.

One day he invited his friends Harry Potter and William Oldres and he lied to them that he has a robot making machine. So they came there to his lab and saw the machine. The two friends went inside and they were happy. But they didn't know that it was a robot copy machine. They were the innocent workers serving in a factory of Tokyo. Robots and the lab were entirely new to them and they were excited as well. When Jinakkafu turned on the machine, the robot parts copied the memory of them and thereby every part attached together and became two humanoid robots with the resemblance of their face. There was a storm and they went inside a ball that took them to the upper side of the lab. They were shocked to see so many humanoid robots with the resemblance of human face. Jinakkafu laughed at their ignorance and was happy as he got two humanoid robots in his collections.

Unaware of Jinakkafu's tricks, Harry and William on the way to their home went to a restaurant and everyone ran away seeing them as they looked grey in colour and behaved strangely.

Harry wondered at the behaviour of the villagers but felt that he couldn't think on his own like before. They went home at last. When they went to their house, wife and kids got scarred. Harry's wife took a frying pan and started to beat Harry. In pain, he screamed "yeh ahhhh", and ran out of the house. He also decided not to come home again. The same happened for William also.

Jinakkafu came to the same restaurant after some time. He wished to see how the villagers react to the persons turned grey in colour. Because he required many human memories to make his humanoid robots. This was observed by Romio, an emerging scientist. He came with his assistant robot to the restaurant and introduced himself. He said that he was a scientist and wished to work with him and control all the robots. Jinakkafu accepted the offer of Romio. Ganma who came over there hated this idea. He intended to be a robot scientist but against the idea of copying memories from humans. He wished to put up a plan otherwise his master will be the robot scientist and he will not get a chance to rule over the robots in Tokyo. So, he immediately went to share this information to his friend Reddio. Reddio was Jinakaffu's enemy and Ganma told about this over phone at night 12 o' clock to him.

Ganma silently went out of Jinakaffu's house and started his scooter to meet Reddio and his friends who were waiting for Ganma. They were so tired when Ganma reached Reddio's house. Reddio opened the gate by hearing the sound of the scooter and informed that everyone was awake. Reddio welcomed, "Come Ganma! We are all in the dining hall." Ganma entered and closed the doors and windows. Then Reddio asked, "Your master got a new partner right!" Ganma answered, "Yes" and Reddio asked the opinion of his friends of how to defeat the plan of the evil scientists. The discussion went on till the morning. Reddio wanted Ganma to tell to his master Jinakaffu, "Boss, you are the best scientist but nobody knows about that. So let us conduct a robot fighting competition. Whoever wins will get a golden robot trophy." Ganma was satisfied by this idea and went home happily.

Ganma informed the idea to Jinakkafu. By hearing this Romio asked Ganma, "Why do you want to conduct a robot competition? It is so strange." Then Ganma explained, "The experiments of my boss are not well established but rather Sunehoro becomes famous indeed." Jinakkafu doesn't mind it at all. But he was happy about Ganma's idea. He assumed,

"Let us organise the robot fighting competition on Saturday at the cricket stadium." He designed the poster for the competition and gave it to Romio's assistant to paste in the important places.

Next morning, Ganma woke up early and went to pick up Reddio and his friends to his lab. The gathered friends were waiting for Ganma and when they hear the honk of Ganma's car all got ready. After an hour, they reached Ganma's lab. There Ganma used the password **Robot Heart Copy**. They went inside and saw the experimental robots.

Ganma showed them the robot copy machine and humanoid robots. He wanted them to choose the robot. They all chose the robots made by Sunehoro and appreciated Ganma for his invention.

Reddio wished to know about the robot control. Ganma replied that all the robots are controlled by the control panel. He also took them to that room and gave them the control panel and he taught how to operate that. They learnt and practised how to compete in the competition. Till the evening they practiced and were satisfied. They wished to come back the next day for much more practice. Ganma after switching off the lights of the room dropped them at their houses and went back to his house to rest.

Next morning, Ganma went again to pick Reddio and his friends to the lab.

Jinakkafu and Romio had a suspicion on Ganma and his activities. So they threw a tracker chip on Ganma. It got struck on his t-shirt. Then Jinakkafu and Romio watched the activities of Ganma in their laptop. Seeing that the Ganma was going to the Reddio's house "Oh no! Ganma was going to Reddio's house", shouted Jinakkafu. Romio asked who that Reddio is. Jinakkafu explained that he is his enemy and narrated his experiences with him. In San Francisco, there was a robot contest in 2020. At that time, he and Reddio participated in that contest. In Level 1, Reddio challenged Jinakkafu and gradually Jinakkafu got defeated. Because of that, Reddio became his enemy. Romio consoled Jinakkafu, "Don't worry; we can make robots with human memory and rule them. So one day we can defeat him as well."

Ganma reached Reddio's house and changed his lab dress. So, the tracker chip got deactivated and Jinakkafu couldn't find the move of Ganma. Ganma and his friends travelled to the lab. When they were travelling, saw the humans who were tired and turned into grey colour. Reddio asked Ganma about them. Everybody got scarred as well. Ganma revealed that his master tricked them and made Humanoid robots by copying their memories. He took them to the room and turned on the lights. He showed the rest of the robot models available in the room. Each one of them selected a model. On the other side of the room, they were able to get the desired robots. They practiced with a boxing doll and went home in the evening. Late in the evening, Sunehoro visited the lab. Due to his weakness he visited the lab occasionally. He desired to cheer up his junior Jinakkafu and chose a robot which he assembled and got ready for the competition.

Ultra Robot fighting competition

CHAPTER TWO

On Saturday at the cricket stadium the participants came with their robots. The announcer started, “Ladies and Gentlemen, Welcome to the ultra robot fighting competition. Hey! Hey! Here is Jinakaffu and here is another fighter Sunehoro. Whoever wins will get a golden trophy and let’s start.” He rang the bell. Jinakaffu clicked the auto weapon. Everyone was shocked by seeing that. He took a weapon and struck Sunehoro’s robot with a single stroke. Sunehoro’s robot was destroyed and all the participants’ robot was destroyed as well. But Sunehoro was happy because he doesn’t know that his junior was envious and a bad scientist. Moreover, he appreciated him for excelling as a great robot scientist. Finally, the last contestant was Reddio. Some encouraged Reddio, the other side of the audience encouraged Jinakaffu. Reddio’s friends worried, “It’s gonna be dangerous. Last time you won him but this time he has alternative weapons and humanoid robots as well,” but Reddio said to his friends not to worry as he can play a game just for fun.

Reddio went and sat with his robot. Jinakaffu warned him and gave him a chance. “Ha Ha last time you won me easily. But now look I came here with alternative weapons and very stronger humanoid robots.” The announcer proclaimed, “Ready Set Go.” Just as he attacked Sunehoro’s robot, Jinakaffu tried to strike Reddio’s robot but Reddio defended the robot by his control panel. The evil robot got up and punched again. Reddio's robot fell down and Jinakaffu tried to harm again with a new weapon. Reddio's robot escaped from that and it fought vigorously. Atlast, Reddio used laser attack and that destroyed Jinakkafu's robot. Jinakkafu cried, "No! No.....It can't be."

Reddio shouted happily, "Oh! Yes. It is." The announcer happily declared the winner. "The winner is Reddio." The audience clapped for Reddio. The announcer gave the golden robot trophy to Reddio. He was so happy and said "Thank you." Jinakaffu was angry about this. Everyone dispersed happily from the cricket stadium after the Ultra robot fighting competition.

Mission of Humanoid Robots

CHAPTER THREE

When everyone dispersed Jinakkafu broke the glasses and other things. By hearing that, Romio came there and said Jinakkafu, "Calm down. What happened! And I think you won. You are a bad guy right." Jinakkafu screamed in anger, "Are you stupid, Have you lost your mind, our robot is just a waste. You said that it is very powerful whereas Reddio's laser attack broke our robot into piece pieces." Romio pacified, "calm down. This is just a little task but remember our master plan." Jinakkafu understood, "Oh! Yes. When are we going to do that Romio?" Romio wished to start on the same day. Jinakkafu thought, "Awesome and he called Ganma..... Ganma." He answered "Yes boss." He got shocked when Jinakkafu asked his help. He said, "Sorry boss. I am too scarred for this mission. So I will be at home." Jinakkafu trusted Ganma and didn't ask anything about his friendship with Reddio. After a while, Jinakkafu and Romio went to the lab. Ganma phoned Reddio and warned him to be careful about his master's plan. Then he alerted his friends too. But Reddio didn't mind that.

Jinakkafu and Romio opened the lab and found 100 humanoid robots which are going to be activated and sent into the city. Romio took the remote from his pocket. Jinakkafu enquired, "What is this remote?" Romio described about the remote. Jinakkafu exclaimed, "Oh! Do it faster. We should destroy the city." Then he clicked a button and the humanoid robots' eyes became red. They got activated and started to walk. Jinakkafu ordered, "Go! Destroy the city. Don't let anybody to escape." Then they started running into the city.

The Breaking News in the media was

"The Humanoid Robots are attacking our city. Who is sending these robots? None can stop these....."

Jinakkafu and Romio laughed by seeing the news Ha Ha Ha Ha Ha...... Romio shouted, "See our humanoid robots are attacking the city." Jinakkafu warned him to be careful as Reddio will do something. He said, "Don't worry. I know the situation. That's why I have sent humanoid robots." Jinakkafu was happy and they went to the lab again.

The Titanic Robot

CHAPTER FOUR

Jinakkafu and Romio went to the control room of the robots. They sat on their chairs. After a while they went to have a look at the city destroyed and damaged. Everywhere they could see their humanoid robots. They saw Reddio's house still not destroyed. So, they got angry and took a bomb and threw on Reddio's house. The house got busted and started to fall. Reddio's friends shouted "Ah! Ah". Reddio calmed them, "Don't worry. I know a place where we can be safe." They escaped and started to run behind Reddio. Seeing that Jinakkafu and Romio laughed, "Ha! Ha! Ha! Run Reddio run and now my robots will take care of you." And they went. Reddio showed his friends a secret tunnel but they got scarred and were not willing to go in. Unwillingly, they went inside. There was a lab and Ganma was sitting there. Reddio's friends asked Ganma, "How it is possible and how did you get here?" Ganma explained, "Actually what happened is, when I informed Reddio, he told me about the secret lab and asked me to come here." Reddio said, "Ok Ok no time for talking. Let's go. I have iron suits for you guys to save from the robots." They all wore it and were happy about their suits. They said the suit was nice and wished to know the plan. Reddio explained, "I have a titanic robot and we are going to go on that only. They are going to fight."

The friends cried out, "Cool awesome." They went to the control room of the lab. They also made the robot fly. When Jinakkafu and Romio saw another robot, they got angry. Then Reddio landed the robot. Jinakkafu shouted, "Reddio....Reddio!!!!"

Reddio told Jinakkafu, "How dare are you to destroy our city?" Then the good robot gave a punch. Evil robot fell on a building. It got up again and fired bullets. Reddio's robot flipped and got escaped. Reddio understood, "Ok you are using bullets. I will use fire balls." The evil robot's hand got damaged but Jinakkafu used another robot hand to fix it and he fixed too. They wrestled for many minutes and at last Reddio remembered the robots match how he defeated Jinakkafu. He used again laser beam then they screamed, "No! No!"

The humanoid robots dismantled. Jinakkafu and Romio realized the situation and escaped in the parachute they had in their lab.

That time inspector of Police came in his jeep. His name was Royston. He was an honest police official who wished to help people of Tokyo. He arrested them after they landed.

Inspector asked them, "Are you making humanoid robots, come to jail and make robots man. I will see, I will see!!" He arrested them and made them to sit in the jeep. He conveyed thanks to the titanic robot. But he wanted the titanic robot to retransfer the copied robots into humans. Titanic robot promised, "Don't worry; I will take care of that. It flew across the city and took the humanoid robots to Reddio's lab and he retransferred robot mind into human mind.

After a few days, humans got their memory and went to their homes happily. Then city became normal again. It became news all over the city.

Breaking News

A titanic robot saved us all and retransferred the memories. Jinakkafu and Romio are in jail. Who sent this titanic robot? Is it the one which saved us from the enemies????

The police found the whereabouts of the titanic robot and understood Reddio and his friends have helped in retransferring human memories from humanoid robots. Reddio and his friends got the ideas and assistance from Dr.Sunehoro too and became superheroes as saved people from enemies. Sunehoro found it difficult to believe about his juniors. But he was happy to help the good scientists. Jinakkafu and Romio listened to all these news in jail.

Jail Birds

CHAPTER FIVE

When Jinakkafu and Romio were in jail, they were shouting and fighting.

They were unhappy because it was years of hard work to get the copy of the memories of humans. Jinakkafu got disappointed as couldn't get the control of the robots in Tokyo. They also got irritated by the food and dress given in the prison. Romio revealed, "We are going to destroy that. Plan A-There is a secret robot file. Plan B- in Reddio's house there is a pen drive lets us take that and replace the duplicate pen drive." Jinakkafu assured, "Don't worry. I have a person to help me. He can get into Reddio's house and replace it." He phoned Shakal and explained what to be done further. After a week, a new scientist came to Tokyo. His name was Shakal. He was a bad scientist known for making robots. His gadgets were so expensive and a mystery to others. He came to Tokyo to see his old friend Ganma who was staying with Reddio now. But his intention is to do bad things and finish what Jinakkafu instructed.

The phone rang in Reddio's house. Kring...... Kring...... Then Ganma attended the phone and asked, "Hello, Ganma here. How could I help you?" Shakal replied, "Hey, Ganma. I am your best friend Shakal. I am coming to your house. I will be there in ten minutes." Ten minutes later he reached. "Ahah.... I reached and should complete the mission," exclaimed Shakal. He rang the calling bell.... ding... dong....Ganma got scared because Shakal will find new wonderful gadgets and end up in danger. Shakal pressed the bell again ding... dong. Reddio asked, "Why are you still here? Open and see who is there." Ganma said, "My old friend scientist Shakal has arrived to the city. He will do so many experiments but with bad intentions. Sometimes in fluke it may end in good." Reddio replied, "Don't be panic. Open the door." Ganma opened the door. Shakal greeted, "Hello, Ganma how are you? I am seeing you after a long time." Ganma was little uneasy. Then Shakal continued, "Hey, Buddy! Why are you nervous? Nah.... doesn't care." Then he asked, "Who is this guy?" Reddio introduced himself, "My name is Reddio." They welcomed him in. He came in and Reddio said to Ganma, "Show him the room," and they went. Shakal refreshed and spoke to Jinakkafu over phone about his successful reach at Reddio's house unaware of Reddio's camera spying him. Ganma went to Reddio's lab. Reddio was thinking deeply over there. Ganma asked, "What are you doing?" Reddio said, "I have a doubt about your old friend. Why he came in the absence of Jinakkafu and Romio? So I have set the camera in his room. Let us see that in the monitor." Then he turned on the monitor and saw what he did in the room. So, they knew that Shakal was a spy prowler. They decided not to take action on Shakal at once.

After a few days, Shakal went somewhere at night without informing anyone. It was a very cold and shivering night. Dogs shouted like wolves. Woooooowowwow.......................

The cats were fighting meow meow...........

Shakal tried to find the way to the prison. He gradually dug an underground tunnel to reach the prison where Jinakkafu and Romio were held. Within a week, the work was complete with the help of some of the henchmen. He decided to rescue Jinakkafu and Romio from the central Jail. So, he went to central jail through the underground tunnel and successfully reached the place. The two police officials who guarded the unit stopped him.

A bodyguard shouted angrily, “Hey Idiot, don’t you know the time. It is midnight. Who are you?” As it was dark, Shakal’s face was not clear. He doesn’t answer anything. Another bodyguard lifted his cane to strike him. Shakal grabbed the cane and kicked him with his leg and pushed him down. The bodyguard got hurt in his head and became unconscious. The other bodyguard yelled, “How dare are you?” and took the gun from his pocket and tried to shoot Shakal. But Shakal slipped and holded the gun and threw it away. He thrashed him terribly. The other bodyguard got hurt as well. Then he went inside the jail with a ball in his hand. He made it to explode and the whole place was filled with smoke. The officials and the guards over there got fainted.

Shakal greeted his friends and released them both with the key hanging in the pocket of the police stood near the prison door. They escaped from there through the same underground tunnel in the prison. Jinakkafu and Romio thanked Shakal for the risk and releasing them from the jail. They went to the house of Romio and stayed over there without the knowledge of others. Shakal promised that he would complete the mission soon. He also got some idea from them for making duplicate pen drive. After that he reached the house of Reddio and behaved sportily accompanying Ganma and his friends. But he was always monitoring the lab of Reddio.

The Acclaimed Robot Scientists

CHAPTER SIX

Breaking News

The two criminals Jinakkafu and Romio escaped from the jail yesterday!!!!!!

A guy with a mask has released them from jail and has hurt two police officials. They are safe now in hospital.

Police would conduct a discreet probe soon.....

By seeing that news, Reddio's friends got scarred. They screamed, "Oh! No. Not again. We thought it was over." Reddio replied them, "Last time we won him and this time too it is possible to win again." Shakal joined with them and said, "I think they will pay back again." Reddio had a doubt on Shakal. Shakal went to his room and started making a duplicate pen drive. He successfully completed and he put the secret ear plugs and spoke to Jinakkafu. He informed about the duplicate pen drive. Jinakkafu said, "Ok. Don't wait. Do it tonight". After a long time at midnight, Shakal secretly rushed out of his room. He kept a dare face like a ghost. He went to Reddio's lab to find the pen drive. He searched everywhere but couldn't get there. Finally, he saw a locker with a lock. He had a spare key and tried to open. He opened with one of the keys he had. When he tried to take the pen drive, the alarm started screaming. Ummmmmmm.......Ummmmmmmmmmmmmm..................

Everybody woke up and came to that lab faster. Shakal broke the glass and escaped. Reddio and his friends searched Shakal. Reddio already kept an eye on him.

Meanwhile, Jinakkafu and Romio were waiting outside the house to get the pen drive from Shakal. When Shakal gave the pen drive Jinakkafu expressed, “Thank You. Shakal. Now I can take over the control of the robots in Tokyo.” At that time, Reddio and his friends found Shakal, Jinakkafu and Romio with the help of the titanic robot. It holded and lifted them up in its arms. The speaker was on. Reddio said, “I know Shakal that you will steal my pen drive. So I already kept a tracker chip.” He snatched the pen drive from them and advised them to be good scientists.

Then the police arrived there. They thanked Reddio and his friends and arrested Shakal, Jinakkafu and Romio. The news spread everywhere.

Reddio, Ganma and Sunehoro made robots legally and used the robots for helping people especially for farming and planting saplings.

He also made people realize that invention of man should be for a good cause and too much of anything is good for nothing.

The End

About The Author

Master S.Shawn Jehafiel is doing his 6 th standard at The Vikasa School, Sawyerpuram, Thoothukudi District, TamilNadu, India. His hobbies are gardening and drawing. He is interested in planting saplings and has planted 20 saplings.

9 798885 461528

Printed by Libri Plureos GmbH in Hamburg,
Germany